Written by
Jane Kurtz

Illustrated by
Claire Messer

CLARA
THE TRIUMPHANT RHINOCEROS

A True Story

BEACH LANE BOOKS
New York   London   Toronto   Sydney   New Delhi

Clara was born in India in 1738.

In the beginning, her life was anything but splendid.

Only a few months old and she was already an orphan.

One small rhinoceros in a big, terrifying world.

Luckily, Clara was taken in by a kind Dutch merchant.
In her new home, she wove around elegant furniture
and ate from dainty plates.
But a rhinoceros is not a pet.
And she was getting bigger every day.

What on earth to do with Clara?

Captain Van der Meer, a visiting sea captain, was fascinated with Clara, and he had an idea.

The 1700s were a time of great curiosity and wonder. Ideas and books were spreading all around Europe. It was an age of questioning and exploring.

People wondered about faraway animals that might live on land or in the sea or sky. Experts had lots of opinions.

◊ THE RHINOCEROS ◊

A rhinoceros, ill-tempered and cruel.

A rhinoceros is fast and cunning, a deadly enemy of elephants.

A rhinoceros has a skin of flowers and armor and ruffles.

A rhinoceros doesn't actually exist!

Captain Van der Meer wanted to take Clara back with him to Europe so people could see for themselves just how wonderful a rhinoceros was.

When his ship left Calcutta, Clara was on board. The sailors covered Clara's sensitive skin with fish oil so it wouldn't dry out or burn in the sun. During the long sea voyage, Captain Van der Meer did all he could to make Clara comfortable.

The two of them became a kind of family.

Six months later, the ship finally reached Rotterdam.

The captain found Clara a pasture in his nearby home of Leiden where she could munch all day. Clara ate and ate and ate, growing bigger, heavier, and stronger than anyone could have imagined.

News about Clara began to spread. Scholars paid to study her. The first picture of her ended up on the cover of a very important scientific book.

After five years, the captain decided it was time for people all over Europe to meet Clara. He just knew he could transport three tons of rhinoceros for thousands of miles on wooden wheels . . .

So off they went!

Through Germany.
　　Through Austria.
　　　　Onward!

Sometimes Clara swept into town in a special carriage pulled by prancing horses. Sometimes swordsmen surrounded the carriage.

To the captain's delight, Clara wasn't seen as a monster. In fact, she was a sensation!

Everybody wanted to meet Clara.

On one trip, Clara floated on the great Rhine River all the way to Switzerland.

How did the captain coax her to get in and out, on and off, up and down?

Oranges.
Clara loved oranges.
She would follow
them everywhere.

This was an age of observing and experimenting, weighing and measuring.

Officials crawled under and around Clara with tapes.

She was gently hoisted into the air by pulleys attached to scales.

It was also an age of kings and queens.

Empress Maria Theresa admired Clara
and shared her amazement with her children.

Clara made her way to France . . .

and visited King Louis XV's menagerie.

In fact, all of Paris fell into Clara-mania!

The women of Paris even created a rhinoceros hairstyle with braids and ribbons.

Since this was an age of art, of course Clara was painted—even life-sized.

Her image was celebrated in words and gleaming ceramics.

Clara was invited to the biggest party in Europe—the Carnival in Venice.

People flocked to see if the rumors they heard were true.

Had Clara drowned on her way to Venice?

(She hadn't.)

Had Clara's horn fallen off?

(It had—but that didn't mean Clara was ill.
In fact, the horn grew back.)

For seventeen years, she met farmers and children, merchants and scientists. One rhinoceros could only be a small piece of the Scientific Revolution.

But Clara changed forever how people thought about her species—
and about other big animals of the land, sky, and sea.

Not cruel and ferocious,
but noble and great.
Not fanciful or ridiculous,
but intelligent and sensitive.

Clara—once so small and alone—
ended her life a triumph,
adored by thousands.

One big rhinoceros in a wide,
welcoming world.

AUTHOR'S NOTE

Though the Dutch sea captain treasured Clara and took the best care of her he could, attitudes toward the keeping of wild animals have thankfully changed dramatically since their time. Today we recognize that rhinos should be in their natural habitat—not confined to a pasture or cage. Yet rhinos (and many, many other wild animal species) still need the help of humans to make sure they are not wiped out.

Today, 260 years since Clara's time, it's even harder for people and rhinos to coexist. The number of Indian rhinos—Clara's species—dropped to fewer than 200 in the wild in the 1950s. Now, thanks to protection and conservation efforts in Assam, India, where Clara was born, there are more than 4,000. Other rhino species are under more pressure. In 2014, when a northern white rhino died at the San Diego Zoo, only five were left alive in the whole world. There are now only two alive, meaning they are essentially extinct. The number of southern white rhinos plunged to only twenty at one point. After a century of conservation efforts, there are about 20,000 southern white rhinos in protected areas and private game reserves, especially in South Africa. Their comeback is a major conservation success story.

Luckily, scientists, conservationists, zookeepers, and others are doing modern-day versions of what the Dutch sea captain did—studying rhinos, figuring out what they need to survive, and sharing knowledge of these magnificent creatures with others. The organization Save the Rhino puts it this way: "If people do not know about these amazing animals and the problems they are facing, how can we expect them to want to do something to help save rhinos?"

ILLUSTRATOR'S NOTE

I first heard of Clara when she was mentioned on an episode of David Attenborough's *Natural Curiosities*. The clip lasted less than two minutes, but from that moment, I was fascinated by Clara and had to find out more!

Imagine being able to see an exotic animal right in front of you, one that most people did not believe even existed. Newspapers at the time reported, "A Rhinoceros is coming to your town, a living Rhinoceros! Such a wonder beast from distant parts has never been seen here before."

Although today we would never want a rhinoceros to live Clara's life, the fact that she traveled the world so extensively for seventeen years is testament to how well the captain looked after her. Clara was very happy in human company, as it was almost all she had ever known. She was a wonderful representative of her species. No wonder Clara enthralled all who met her!

Clara and the Wonder Cabinet

Cabinets of curiosities, or "wonder cabinets" as they became known, were very popular in the eighteenth century as showcases of the owners' worldly knowledge and displays of wealth. Clara inspired an extensive range of memorabilia that could have easily filled many wonder cabinets!

Here are some Clara artifacts that still survive today:

1) Louis XV ormolu musical clock, by Jean-Joseph de Saint-Germain, Paris, France

2) Dinnerware service, Meissen, Germany

3) Cast bronze rhinoceros, perhaps Mannheim, Germany, or Ghent, Belgium (The Barber Institute of Fine Arts, Birmingham, England, and The Victoria and Albert Museum, London, England)

4) Denis Diderot and Jean le Rond d'Alembert's *Encyclopédie* (1751–72) and Georges-Louis Leclerc, Comte de Buffon's *Histoire Naturelle* (1749–1804)

5) Dinnerware service, Meissen, Germany

6) Decorative medal commissioned by Captain Van der Meer to celebrate Clara's arrival in a new city

7) White marble rhinoceros, by Augustin-Bernard-François Portois, probably Ghent, Belgium (The Bowes Museum)

For Rebekah,
who woke me up at Treetops Hotel in Kenya
to see a rhino at the water hole and who is now
my eighteenth-century specialist.
—J. K.

For Jamie—stay wild.
And for Luca, who waited very patiently to be born
whilst I finished this book.
—C. M.

Selected Sources and Further Reading

Hewitt, Sarah. *Clara: The True Story of Clara the Rhino*. London: Books By Sarah Publishing, 2016.

Holmes, Mary. *My Travels with Clara*. Los Angeles: J. Paul Getty Museum, 2007.

McCully, Emily Arnold. *Clara: The (Mostly) True Story of the Rhinoceros Who Dazzled Kings, Inspired Artists, and Won the Hearts of Everyone . . . While She Ate Her Way Up and Down a Continent*. New York: Schwartz & Wade Books, 2016.

Ridley, Glynis. *Clara's Grand Tour: Travels with a Rhinoceros in Eighteenth-Century Europe*. New York: Grove Atlantic, 2004.

van der Ham, Gijs. *Clara the Rhinoceros*. Rotterdam: nai010, 2022.

Save the Rhino International: savetherhino.org.

To learn more about Clara, visit janekurtz.com.

BEACH LANE BOOKS • An imprint of Simon & Schuster Children's Publishing Division • 1230 Avenue of the Americas, New York, New York 10020 • Text © 2025 by Jane Kurtz • Illustration © 2025 by Claire Messer • Book design by Lauren Rille • All rights reserved, including the right of reproduction in whole or in part in any form. • BEACH LANE BOOKS and colophon are trademarks of Simon & Schuster, LLC. • For information about special discounts for bulk purchases, please contact Simon & Schuster Special Sales at 1-866-506-1949 or business@simonandschuster.com. • The Simon & Schuster Speakers Bureau can bring authors to your live event. For more information or to book an event, contact the Simon & Schuster Speakers Bureau at 1-866-248-3049 or visit our website at www.simonspeakers.com. • The text for this book was set in Geographica. • The illustrations in this book were rendered by printing linoleum blocks in black ink, then applying color digitally. • Manufactured in China • 1224 SCP • First Edition • 10 9 8 7 6 5 4 3 2 1 • Library of Congress Cataloging-in-Publication Data • Names: Kurtz, Jane, author. | Messer, Claire, illustrator. • Title: The triumphant rhinoceros / Jane Kurtz ; illustrated by Claire Messer. • Description: First edition. | New York : Beach Lane Books, 2025. | Includes bibliographical references. | Audience: Ages 4–8. | Audience: Grades 2–3. | Summary: Captain Van der Meer turns an orphaned rhinoceros named Clara into a sensation, traveling all over Europe and changing how people think about her species. Based on a true story. Includes author's note. • Identifiers: LCCN 2022008069 (print) | LCCN 2022008070 (ebook) | ISBN 9781481467032 (hardcover) | ISBN 9781481467049 (ebook) • Subjects: LCSH: Rhinoceroses—Juvenile fiction. | CYAC: Rhinoceroses—Fiction. | Human-animal relationships—Fiction. | Europe—History—1648–1789—Fiction. • Classification: LCC PZ10.3.K9735 Tr 2023 (print) | LCC PZ10.3.K9735 (ebook) | DDC [E]—dc23 • LC record available at https://lccn.loc.gov/2022008069 • LC ebook record available at https://lccn.loc.gov/2022008070